D1211642

My Favorite Book

Lessons To Grow On

A book about giving, learning lessons, and growing up

Good Will, Inc.

The lessons that help children grow...

We all learn life's lessons best through experience. This is especially true for children. *My Favorite Book* is the story of a child's experiences in growth. It can be used as a springboard for discussion between parent and child and teacher and child.

During the primary school years, a child's world expands beyond the home to include the school and the community. *My Favorite Book* has sections on the home, on the school and on the community, because these are important environments in which the child learns.

The lessons that help children grow should be very positive ones. Reading is one of these experiences. Talking about what he or she reads is another. Learning about the community is still another.

The community leaders who sponsor *My Favorite Book* are proud to play a role in providing these learning experiences for the children in your community. Their names appear on the opposite page.

Good Will Publishers
P.O. Box 269
Gastonia, NC 28053

My Favorite Book

Sponsored by

MAY THIS ALWAYS BE
YOUR FAVORITE BOOK

This is *My Favorite Book.*

Put your picture here

This is me.

Ryan Freeman

This is my name.

2752284

This is my telephone number.

408 Sunny Lane, Dublin, Ga

This is my address.

Mom calls me Timothy.
Dad calls me Tim.

COMICS

Grandpa calls me Timmy,
and I agree with him.

I have a sister named Mary Jo.
Sometimes she's bossy.
I told her so.

She shook her head
and grinned and said,
"Look in the fridge
and see for me
if the fudge is hard yet."

The fudge was on the top shelf.
My head is not that high
so I reached up to pull it down.
"Oh me
Oh me
Oh my!"

Sister didn't yell at me.
She asked if I was hurt.
And Sadie my dog
saw her chance…

to get a quick dessert.

Grandpa said that growing up can be hard.
"But if you do the best you can,
and be the best you can be,
life can also be sweet.

Just like sister's fudge,
life can be hard *and* sweet."

I feed Sadie,
and my room is neat.
On top of that
Mom says I'm sweet.
I even try to eat
green beans.
I *think* I know
what Grandpa means

On Thanksgiving Day
my family gets bigger
with aunts and uncles
and cousins and friends.
So, if I'm asked the size
of my family,
I say, "Well, it just depends."

Bonnie Lee's my next-door-neighbor.
It's fun when we're together.
We help each other do our chores.
We're friends now and forever.

At night Mom tucks me in
and reads to me.
She tells me stories too.
Like how my dad
was Grandpa's boy
and brought him joy
like I now do.

I love my family and they love me
even though I spilled the fudge.

TURN THE PAGE TO GO TO SCHOOL.

I go to school
most every day.
I feel at home
even though I'm away.

Miss Grant, my teacher, tells us about
the world we're in
and the world on a map.
She teaches us words and so much more.
Like numbers and adding 1, 2, 3, 4…

She makes us feel that we've something to give,
and we'll love Miss Grant as long as we live.

My class has lots of children
so we've all learned to share.
We share our toys.
We share our thoughts.
By sharing, we show we care.

We also try to listen
and take our turns to speak.
It's harder for some than others.
Some mouths just seem to leak.

One of the things I like to do
is to go outside and play.
If the weather is good
and our work is done,
we do it most every day.

I like to win the games we play,
and lots of times I do.
Like climbing on the jungle gym
and tag and dodge ball too.

There is a large old oak tree
just off our school yard grounds.
Miss Grant said not to climb that tree.
"That tree is out of bounds!"

Jason dared me to climb the oak.
He said he thought I couldn't.
When school let out, I climbed that tree
knowing that I shouldn't.

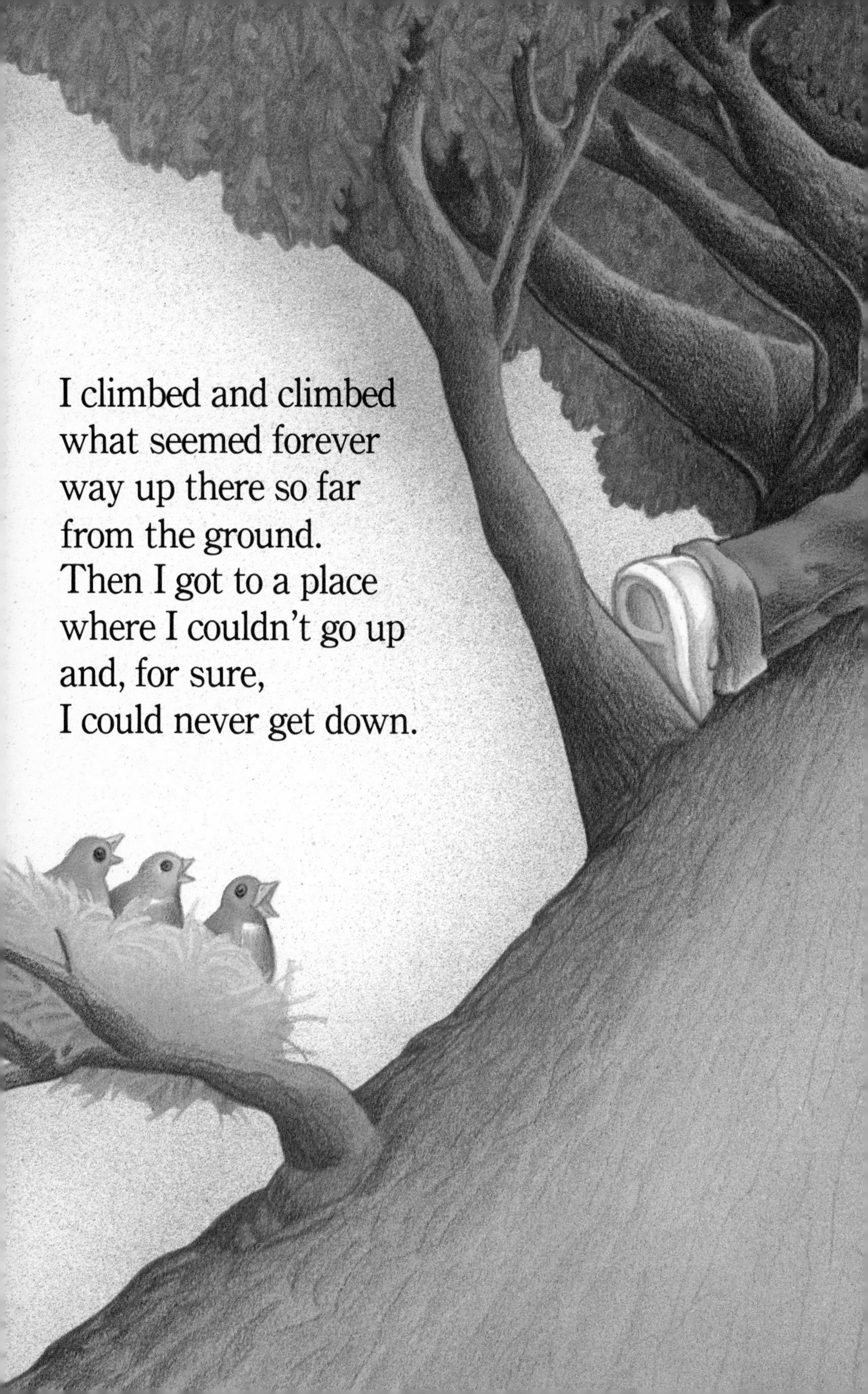

I climbed and climbed
what seemed forever
way up there so far
from the ground.
Then I got to a place
where I couldn't go up
and, for sure,
I could never get down.

When I looked around,
Jason was gone.
I felt as scared as could be.
Was there no one there
to get me down?
"Oh, what's going to
happen to me?"

Just when I thought I would never be saved,
Bonnie Lee brought Miss Grant outside.
Miss Grant said the ladder
would not reach where I was
so I stayed there alone and cried.

I waited for the fireman
in that old oak tree.
Oh, how foolish I'd been.
I had taken that dare
and had gone out of bounds
just to prove I could win.

But winning's not climbing to the tops of trees
when you have no way to get down.
The fireman said that *birds* live in trees,
and I'd better stay on the ground.

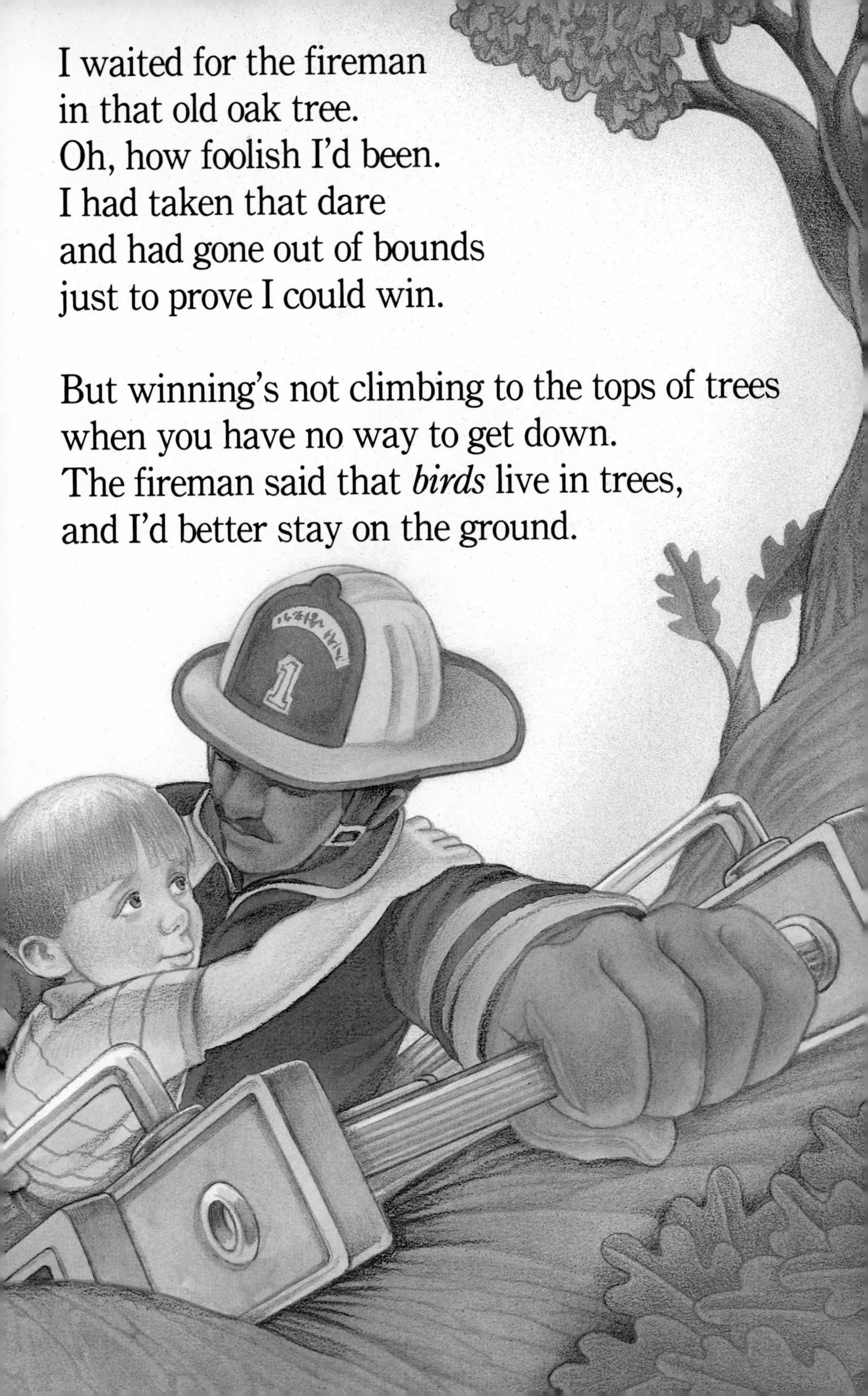

"Timmy, you've given us all such a scare!"
Miss Grant was upset.
Boy, I blew it.
"The rules that we have are
because we care."
She was so right
and I knew it.

What a friend Bonnie Lee had been to me!
I think she was very brave.
The fireman and principal said she was special.
They asked her to help me behave!

TURN THE PAGE TO GO DOWNTOWN.

One day we took a ride downtown
and, on the way, passed a cornfield.
Grandpa said that the field was important.
A cornfield is how we get corn meal.

Corn flakes and corn bread and corn-on-the-cob
are brought by the farmers who are doing their job.

My dad explained to Bonnie Lee and me
what it means to live in a community.

"It's where churches and schools
and businesses too
care about people through
the jobs that they do."

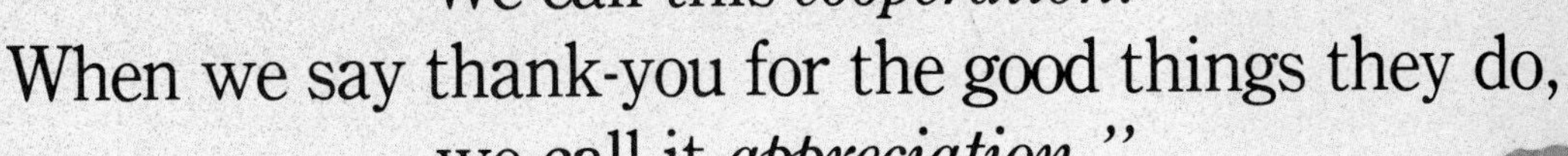

Grandpa said, "Our town works together.
We call this *cooperation*.
When we say thank-you for the good things they do,
we call it *appreciation*."

Our last stop in town
was the grocery store
where Grandpa
bought us a treat.

He carried a bag
that was full
of something.
We hoped it was
something sweet.

He opened the bag.
We looked inside.

There sat the yummiest fudge.
Mounds upon mounds all solid and square.
Then Grandpa gave me a nudge.

"Some lessons are hard, Timmy.
You know that is true.
But some lessons are easy
like the good that people do.
Now taste your fudge.
Is it hard and sweet?"

Then my grandpa winked at me,
and Bonnie Lee looked confused.
So I told her what happened when I spilled the fudge,
while grandpa looked amused.

“Spilling fudge and breaking rules
were very hard lessons I’d say!
But getting a treat and having you as my friend
are lessons in just the same way.

So some lessons are hard like this piece of fudge.”
I smiled as I started to eat.
“All the lessons we learn make our lives so much better.
Then life can be oh so sweet.”

THE END